To my daughters, Mina & Leah

mai5　naa4　ge3　sam1　cing4　bat1　gei3

米娜嘅心情筆記
MINA'S UPS & DOWNS

For a FREE audio reading and other bilingual books visit:

www.lycheepress.com

Scan to listen to the audio reading!

Follow

@minalearnschinese

Translation by
Cantonese Mommy, Tracy Ng, and Cody Cheung

Also available in Mandarin Editions in Traditional or Simplified Chinese!

ISBN: 979-8-89111-002-1

gam1 jat6 hai6 ngo5 dai6 jat1 ci3 lai4 gaa1 nin4 waa4! m4 zi1 ni1 dou6 hai6 dim2 ge3 ne1?

今日係我第一次嚟嘉年華！唔知呢度係點嘅呢？

Today is my first time at a Carnival! I wonder what it would be like?

ngo5 hou2 hou3 kei4 aa3.

我 好 好 奇 呀 。

I'm feeling curious.

lai4 tai2 haa5 fuk1 dei6 tou4.　　waa1!　　jau5 gam3 do1 hou2 waan2 ge3 je5!　　ngo5 hou2 hing1 fan5!

嚟睇吓幅地圖。哇！有咁多好玩嘅嘢！我好興奮！

Let's look at the map. Wow, so many fun things to do. I'm really excited!

aa1!　　　tai2　lok6 heoi3 taai3 gou1 laa1!　　　ngo5 hou2 geng1 aa1!

啊！睇落去太高啦！我好驚啊！

Ah! That looks too high! I'm so scared!

mai5 naa4,　　 ngo5　zi1　dou6 nei5　jau5　di1 gan2 zoeng1,　daan6 hai6 m4 sai2 daam1 sam1 gaa3.

米娜，我知道你有啲緊張，但係唔洗擔心㗎。

Mina, I know you're feeling a little nervous, but don't worry.

jat1 ding6 wui5 hou2 ci3　gik1,　　 hou2 hou2 waan2 ge3.

一定會好刺激，好好玩嘅 。

It will be so much fun.

hai6　si4　hau6　kau3 hou2 on1 cyun4 daai3 laa1!　　maa1 mi4 gong2 dak1 ngaam1,

係時候扣好安全帶啦！媽咪講得啱，

Time to buckle up! Mommy is right.

ngo5　jat1　ding6 dak1 ge3!　　ngo5 hou2 daai6 daam2 gaa3.

我一定得嘅！我好大膽㗎。

I can do this! I'm feeling brave.

tai2 haa5 ngo5!　　　ngo5 hai2 hou2 gou1 hou2 gou1 ge3 tin1 hung1 soeng6 min6 fei1 gan2 aa3!

睇吓我！ 我喺好高好高嘅天空上面飛緊呀！

Look at me! I'm flying so high in the sky!

hou2 ci3 gik1 aa3!

好刺激呀！

It's thrilling!

ngo5 zeon2 bei6 heoi3 tiu1 zin3 haa5 zo6 gwo3 saan1 ce1 aa3.

我 準 備 去 挑 戰 吓 坐 過 山 車 呀 。

I'm ready to try the big roller coaster now.

ngo5 hou2 jau5 seon3 sam1!

我 好 有 信 心 ！

I'm feeling confident!

daan6 hai6 ngo5 taai3 ai2 laa3!

但係我太矮喇！

But I'm too short!

ngo5 zan1 hai6 hou2 soeng2 zo6 ni1 gaa3 gwo3 saan1 ce1 aa3!

我真係好想坐呢架過山車呀！

I really wanted to ride the roller coaster. I feel so heartbroken!

ngo5 hou2 soeng1 sam1 aa3!

我好傷心呀！

I feel so heartbroken!

ngo5 yun4 bun2 soeng2 ke4 coeng4 geng2 luk2 gaa3,

我原本想騎長頸鹿㗎，

I wanted to ride the giraffe,

daan6 hai6 ji5 ging1 jau5 jan4 ke4 gan2 laa3.

但係已經有人騎緊喇。

but it's already taken.

ngo5 hou2 sat1 mong6 aa3!

我好失望呀！

I'm so disappointed!

dang2 zan6,　　go2 zek3 hai6 mai6 duk6 gok3 sau3 lai4 gaa3?

等陣，嗰隻係咪獨角獸嚟㗎？

Wait, is that a unicorn?

ni1　dou6 ging2 jin4　jau5　ngo5 zeoi3 zung1 ji3　ge3 dung6 mat6!

呢度竟然有我最鍾意嘅動物！

I can't believe they have my favorite animal!

ngo5 hou2 ging1 ngaa2 aa3!

我好驚訝呀！

I'm so surprised!

syut3 gou1,　　bok6 beng2,　　min4 faa1 tong2,

雪糕、薄餅、棉花糖、

jit6 gau2,　　ziu1 tong4 ping4 gwo2, paau3 guk1,

熱狗、焦糖蘋果、爆谷、

tung4 ning4 mung1 seoi2.　　ngo5　m4　zi1　sik6 bin1 joeng6

同檸檬水。 我唔知食邊樣

hou2 tim1.　　ngo5 dou1 m4　zi1 dim2 gaan2 hou2.

好添，我都唔知點揀好。

Ice cream, pizza, cotton candy, hot dogs, candy apples, popcorn and lemonade. I can't decide what to eat. I'm feeling torn.

ngo5 tou5 ngo6 laa3!　　zan1 hai6 hou2 hou2 mei6 aa3!

我肚餓喇！　真係好好味呀！

I'm hungry! Yummy!

ngo5 dei6 sik6 jyun4 faan6 hau6 ho2 m4 ho2 ji5 heoi3 can1 can1 dung6 mat6 jyun4 aa3?

我哋食完飯後可唔可以去親親動物園呀？

Can we visit the petting zoo after lunch?

ni1　di1　gam3 dak6 bit6　ge3　je5　sik6　m4
呢啲咁特別嘅嘢食唔
hai6　jat6　jat6　dou1 sik6　dou3 gaa3!
係日日都食到㗎！
It's not every day that I get to eat these special treats.

ngo5 zan1 hai6 hang6 fuk1 aa3!
我真係幸福呀！
I'm so lucky!

好煩呀！我好嬲！

hou2 faan4 aa3! ngo5 hou2 nau1!

So annoying! I'm so angry!

ne1　go3　jau4　hei3 ge3 zoeng2 ban2 hai6　zek3 hou2 zeng3 ge3 wu1 gwai1 gung1 zai2.

呢 個 遊 戲 嘅 獎 品 係 隻 好 正 嘅 烏 龜 公 仔 。

ngo5 dou1 soeng2 jing4　jat1　zek3　aa3!

我 都 想 贏 一 隻 呀 !

This game has a really cool turtle! I hope I can win one!

ngo5 daa2 m4 zung3 aa3!　taai3 naan4 laa3.

我打唔中呀！太難喇。

ngo5 hou2 m4 hoi1 sam1!

我好唔開心！

I missed! It's too hard. I'm so sad!

ngo5 zi1　nei5 jau5　di1　sat1 lok6,　bat1 gwo3 nei5 zung6 jau5 jat1 ci3　gei1 wui6 ga3 ma4.　gaa1 jau2!

我知你有啲失落，不過你仲有一次機會㗎嘛。加油！

I know you're feeling frustrated, but you still have another chance. You've got this!

hou2 ge3!　　gam1 ci3 ngo5 wui2 nou5 lik6 di1 miu4 zeon2 go3 muk6 biu1.　　Ngo5 hou2 jau5 kyut3 sam1gaa3。

好嘅！今次我會努力啲瞄準個目標。我好有決心㗎。

Okay! I'll concentrate harder this time. I'm determined.

ngo5 dak1 zo2 laa3!

我得咗喇！

I did it!

ngo5 jeng4 zo2 daai6 zoeng2 aa3!

我贏咗大獎呀！

ngo5 hou2 zi6　hou4 aa1!

我好自豪啊！

I won the big prize! I'm feeling so proud of myself.

hai6 duk6 gok3 sau3 hei3 kau4 aa3!

係獨角獸氣球呀！

de1 di4 maa4 maa1 do1 ze6 nei5 dei6 aa1！

爹哋媽咪多謝你哋呀！

gam1 jat6 zan1 hai6 taai3 jyun4 mei5 laa3!

今日真係太完美喇！

ngo5 hou2 gam2 yan1!

我好感恩！

A unicorn balloon! Daddy, Mommy, thank you!
This is the best day ever! I feel grateful!

Visit Lycheepress.com and check out these
other books in Cantonese by Katrina Liu

Hi! If you enjoyed this book, please consider leaving an
honest review. Your support will allow me to continue
creating stories in Cantonese. Thank you! — Katrina

Made in United States
Orlando, FL
26 February 2024